KING OF THE SWAMP

For my lovely boys, Jude, Flynn and
Archie and for my lovely husband,
who always believed in McDarkly - CE

For Maeve Ann Hood - BM

SIMON & SCHUSTER
First published in Great Britain in 2020 by Simon & Schuster UK Ltd
1st Floor, 222 Gray's Inn Road, London, WC1X 8HB
Text copyright © 2020 Catherine Emmett · Illustrations copyright © 2020 Benjamin
Mantle · The right of Catherine Emmett and Benjamin Mantle to be identified as the
author and illustrator of this work has been asserted by her in accordance with the
Copyright, Designs and Patents Act, 1988 · All rights reserved, including the right of
reproduction in whole or in part in any form · A CIP catalogue record for this book is
available from the British Library upon request.
978-1-4711-8170-2 (HB) · 978-1-4711-8169-6 (PB) · 978-1-4711-8171-9 (EB)
Printed in China · 10 9 8 7 6 5 4 3 2

KING OF THE SWAMP

CATHERINE EMMETT

BEN MANTLE

SIMON & SCHUSTER
London   New York   Sydney   Toronto   New Delhi

The swamp was quite dark
and the swamp was quite dank,
And due to the mud,
the swamp really quite stank.

McDarkly lived quietly, all on his own,
And dreamed of transforming his muddy swamp home.

He had a neat garden,
which had a neat wall,

Some flowers were spotted,
some flowers were plain,

Each year he grew orchids,
some large and some small.

McDarkly, he cherished
them all just the same.

One day, as he tended a tiny new bud,
He heard lots of 'someones' all ride
through the mud . . .

"This here's where I'll build my new roller skate park!
I'll concrete it all 'cos it's stinky and dark.

Oh look over there, at that strange,
swampy thing! Yes! YOU! Stinky creature,
bow down to your King!"

The King and his minions all started to laugh,
"Oh, call for my butler to give *it* a bath!"

"No, no!" cried McDarkly, "The orchids will die!"
He wrung both his hands and he stammered a cry,
"If you could just look at their b-b-beauty . . . their g-g-race
You'd see that the swamp is a m-m-magical place."

The Princess rode forward, "Grow orchids you say?
They'd help with my research, do show me the way!"

McDarkly said sadly, "They've not flowered yet . . .
In a c-c-couple of weeks you will love 'em I bet!"

"Oh Daddy, I have to insist we return,
Just think of the marvellous
things I could learn!"

"Alright" huffed the King. "We return in ten days!"
He scowled at McDarkly, "Now buck up your ways!
The WHOLE of this swamp best be bursting with grace,
Or soon I'll be skating all over this place!"

The next day McDarkly
was up before dawn,
He rubbed at his eyes
and he stifled a yawn.

He gathered the plants and
the tools he would need,
His swamp was at stake
so he **HAD** to succeed!

He shovelled the mud 'til
his shoulders were sore,
Then shovelled and planted
and shovelled some more.

The light was soon fading,
the sun was soon set,
McDarkly kept going!
He couldn't stop yet!

He worked without ceasing and time flew so fast,
That quickly he found that his ten days had passed ...
But as he was singing his flowering song,

He spotted a 'something' that didn't belong ...

Right there on the leaf
of a small prickly shrub,
He spotted a tiny and
furry, green grub!

McDarkly was panicked! But what could he do?
He thought for a moment and then he said "**SHOOO!**"
But just as he lifted it off with his paw,
He looked all around and he saw there were . . .

His stomach was churning,
he felt rather sick!
He had to do something
and do something quick!

He tried to remove them
as fast as he could,
But there were so many –
it didn't look good!

His flowers were eaten in one single night
And nothing was left, no, not one single bite.

His swamp would be lost and he tried not to cry.
He knew he had failed and he howled at the sky.

The horses and riders returned the next day,
McDarkly said nothing, for what could he say?
But just as the King was guffawing in glee,

The Princess exclaimed,

"Oh my, good gracious me!

Why look at the beauty and look at the grace!
This really is quite the most magical place!"

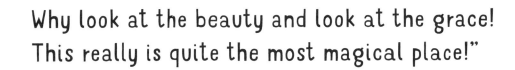

McDarkly turned round to see what she had seen,
And there, where his poor ruined orchids had been,
There weren't any furry, green grubby-like things,

But hundreds of butterflies
fluttered their wings!

The Princess excitedly made a decree,
"This place from now on is protected by me!
This swamp is the first of my nature reserves.
McDarkly will run it, it's what he deserves."

McDarkly stood silent – inside his heart soared!
He knew he had rescued the swamp he adored.

From then on the pair of them often would meet.
She found him some orchids the grubs would not eat.

The plans that they made
were so splendid and grand,
The Princess decided he
needed a hand.

It turned out the King had some butlers to spare,

In fact before long, she had **HIM** working there!

The swamp was still dank, but no longer so dark,
And never became the King's roller skate park.

McDarkly had proven that beauty and grace,
Can sometimes be found in the stinkiest place.